Puppy in my Pocket

SCHOLASTIC READER
LEVEL 3
700-1500 WORDS

Water Pups

D1243301

By Sierra Harimann
Illustrated by The Artifact Group

SCHOLASTIC INC.

ISBN 978-0-545-47235-7

Published by Scholastic Inc. SCHOLASTIC and associated logos are trademarks and/or registered trademarks of Scholastic Inc.
Lexile is a registered trademark of MetaMetrics, Inc.

12 11 10 9 8 7 6 5 4 3 2 1   13 14 15 16 17 18/0

Designed by Angela Jun

Printed in the U.S.A.   40

First printing, April 2013

It was the first day of summer vacation, and the puppies were going to the Puppyville Swim Club.

"I love summer!" Montana barked happily. "We'll have two whole months of fun in the sun at the pool."

"This summer I'm *finally* going to jump off the high diving board," Spike told his friends as they headed to the club.

"Good for you, Spike!" Montana yipped. "We'll be cheering for you. Right, Gigi?"

"*Mais oui,*" Gigi replied. "Of course!"

2

As the puppies were walking, they saw their friends Charo and Peanut.

"Hi!" Montana greeted them. "Are you on your way to the pool, too?"

Charo nodded and smiled, but Peanut didn't look so happy.

"What's wrong, Peanut?" Gigi asked as she put her towel on a chair. "It's summer vacation, and we're at the pool!"

Peanut sighed. "I know," he barked softly. "But I'm afraid of the water. And I don't know how to swim. I'll just dip my paws in."

"Your paws?" Gigi asked. "That's no fun! Why don't I teach you to swim?"

"I can help, too," Montana added. "You'll have all summer to practice."

"Really?" Peanut asked shyly. "You two would do that for me?"

"*Mais oui!*" Gigi cried. "That's what friends are for."

"Come on, Peanut," Gigi said as she headed for the pool. "Time for your first lesson!"

Peanut looked scared.

"R-right n-n-now?" he stuttered. "But we just got here. Shouldn't we wait a little while for the water to warm up?"

"Nope," Montana barked gently. "The best way to get over your fear is to dive right in! The secret is to not even think about it. See?"

With that, Montana hopped right into the pool.

"Well, maybe not *dive* right in," Gigi said as she trotted into the pool. "It's okay to use the ramp."

Peanut dipped his paw into the pool and pulled it out, wincing.

"Come on, Peanut," Montana urged gently. "It's shallow here, so you'll still be able to stand up."

"You can do it," Gigi added.

Peanut took a deep breath and slowly made his way into the pool.

"Yay!" Montana said. "That's the hardest part. Now that you're in the pool, let's try doggie paddling."

Montana showed Peanut how to move his front paws through the water.

Peanut tried his best, but he ended up swallowing some water.

"*Blech!*" Peanut spluttered. Then he scampered back up the ramp and out of the pool. "Thanks for the lesson, guys, but I'm done for the day. I decided I don't really want to learn how to swim after all."

"Are you sure, Peanut?" Gigi asked gently from the pool. "Everyone swallows some water the first time."

"Yup," Peanut replied. "I'm just going to sit in this chair and read my favorite book."

"Well, okay," Montana replied reluctantly. "But let us know if you change your mind."

Meanwhile, at the other end of the pool, Spike was trying to muster the courage to jump off the high diving board.

You can do it, Spike thought to himself as he tiptoed to the edge of the board. *But it's such a long way down!*

Peanut watched Gigi and Montana playing in the pool. He really *did* want to learn to swim, but he was too scared.

Just then, Charo came over to get her towel.

14

"Hey, Peanut," she said. "Want to watch Spike jump off the high diving board with me? We can cheer him on."

"Sure," Peanut agreed. Watching Spike sounded like more fun than sitting alone on the pool deck.

"What happened?" Charo asked as Spike climbed back down the ladder. "I thought you were going to jump."

"I changed my mind," Spike replied gruffly.

"Are you afraid?" Peanut asked. "That diving board is really high!"

"I'm not afraid," Spike replied, puffing out his chest. "I just don't want to jump anymore. I'm hungry."

"Okay," Peanut replied with a shrug. "Let's go get lunch."

"I'm going to swim a little more first," Charo told her friends. "See you later!"

"I know you're not afraid, but I would be," Peanut told Spike over peanut butter and jelly sandwiches. "I'm scared to even get in the pool and do the doggie paddle."

He sighed sadly.

"Try thinking of the pool like a great big bathtub," Spike told his friend. "Then it will be less scary."

"You're right," Peanut said. "Montana says the best way to get over my fear is to dive right in without even thinking about it. But it's not as easy as it sounds."

Spike was quiet for a minute. Then he suddenly realized something.

"Maybe it *is* as easy as it sounds!" he told Peanut. "Come on, I'll show you!"

Spike headed straight for the high diving board as Peanut watched, his eyes wide.

Spike scampered up the ladder. Without even pausing, he ran to the edge of the diving board.

"Wheeeeeee!" he shouted as he jumped.

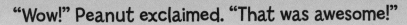

"Wow!" Peanut exclaimed. "That was awesome!"

"Way to go, Spike," Montana barked.

"Oui!" cried Gigi. "That was incredible!"

"Amazing!" Charo agreed.

Spike climbed out of the pool and took a bow.

"Thanks, guys," Spike told his friends. "And thanks for your advice, Montana."

"What advice?" Montana asked, confused.

"You told Peanut that the best way to get over his fear of the water was to just jump in without stopping to think about it," Spike explained. "So that's what I did!"

"I know I said I wasn't afraid, Peanut," Spike told his friend. "But I was. Talking with you really helped me, though."

"It did?" Peanut asked, surprised.

Spike nodded. "I wanted to show you that it's possible to do something even if you're scared."

Peanut thought for a moment, and then turned to Montana and Gigi.

"I think I'm ready for my next swimming lesson," he said.

"Great!" Gigi cried. "Let's get in the pool!"

"Okay, here goes," Peanut said bravely as he dashed down the ramp into the water.

"*Magnifique!*" Gigi agreed. "Great job!"

"Let's use a kickboard this time," Montana suggested. "Just hold on to the board and it will help you float. Then kick your back paws and you'll move forward."

Peanut took a kickboard from Montana and gave it a try. He tried to move in a straight line, but every time he kicked, he went to one side of the lane or the other.

"That's okay, you're doing fine!" Montana barked encouragingly. "Learning something new takes time. You'll get the hang of it."

Peanut kept kicking. He moved back and forth across the pool. By his fourth lap he was kicking in a straight line!

"I did it!" Peanut yelped proudly.

Across the pool, Spike continued to practice jumping off the high diving board.

"*Cannonball!*" Spike shouted happily before he splashed into the water.

Peanut and Spike gave each other a high five.

"Way to go, Spike!" Peanut said.

"You, too!" Spike replied. "We're the bravest puppies around!"